Little Bears go to School

Heather Maisner

Illustrated by
Tomislav Zlatic

W

FRANKLIN WATTS
LONDON • SYDNEY

Evie

Hello. I'm Big Bear. The little bears are going to school and I'm helping out today. Little Evie Bear has come with me but she likes playing hide-and-seek.

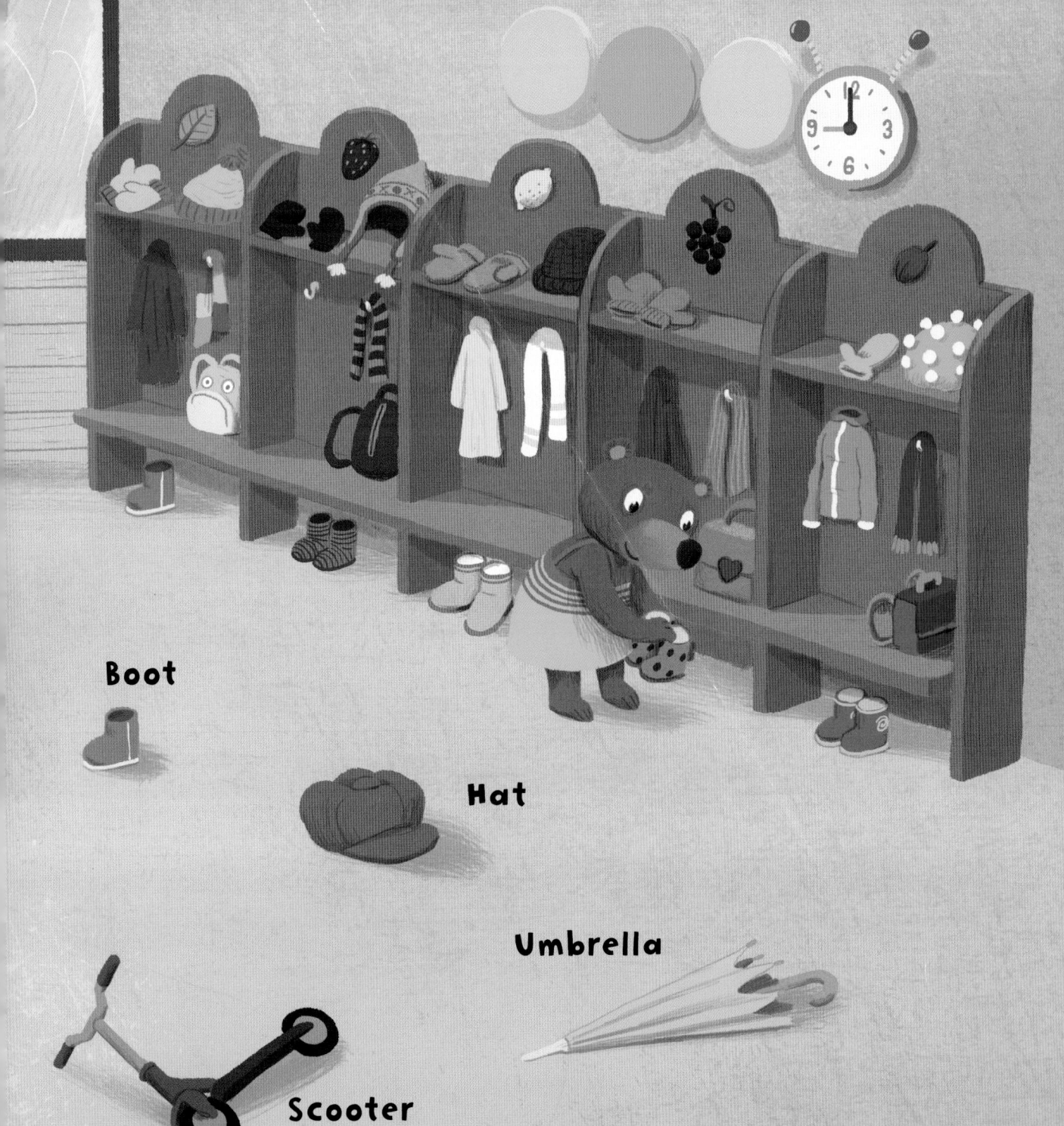

Boot

Hat

Umbrella

Scooter

Thank you. Now where is little Evie Bear?
And did you see something flutter by?

A butterfly flew in while we were busy. Can you see it? And can you see the worm that wriggled in from the garden?

Puzzle
piece

Pencil

Scissors

Now we're in the reading and writing
corner. What a messy corner it is!
Where do all these things belong?

Map

Shape   **Ruler**

Building block

Book

That's better. Can you find little Evie Bear? I think I saw the school kitten jump in through the window. Can you see her?

And can you find the little blue collar with a bell that she was wearing round her neck?

Doll

Now we're in the home corner. Just look how many things there are to put away!

Fancy dress

Pan

Knife and fork

Weights

Teddy

Milk

Blanket

Well done.
Oh no, the
school budgie has escaped
from his cage! And I think I
saw a caterpillar crawling about.

Can you find them both, please?
And where is little Evie Bear?

Jug

Sponge

Fish

We're in the water and sand corner now and things are toppling about all over the place. We really need to put them back neatly.

Bucket

Camel

Plant

Boat

Spade

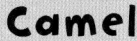

Things are definitely looking better.
I wonder where Evie Bear is hiding?
And did you hear that clucking sound?

The school chicken is running around and
and I think she's laid an egg. Can you find
the chicken and her egg, please?

Paper

Here we are in the painting corner. It's very untidy. Where do you think these things should go?

Apron

Glue

Paint brush

Paint lid

Crayon

Picture

That's much better. But now the school hamster has escaped from his cage and a snail has crawled in from the playground.

Can you spot them both and can you find Evie Bear?

Hamster

Chicken

All my little bears are having fun in the playground. But now it is time to line up to go home. Please give each little bear the correct hat and scarf.

Dog

Budgie

Kitten

And please put each pet in the correct place.

Well done!
But a frog and a
duck just leapt out
of the school pond.

Can you spot them both?

Home at last! The school is tidy and all the little bears and the school pets are safely asleep. I do hope you'll come and see us again.